JONAH'S Kiss

Jonah's Kiss

Naomi Springthorp

Jonah's Kiss
Copyright © 2021 Naomi Springthorp
Published by Love & Devotion Author Services, Inc.
All rights reserved

Print Edition ISBN 978-1-949243-59-8

Jonah's Kiss is a work of fiction and does not in any way advocate irresponsible behavior. This book contains content that is not suitable for readers 17 and under. Please store your files where they cannot be accessed by minors.

Any resemblance to actual things, events, locales, or persons living or dead is entirely coincidental. Names, characters, places, brands, products, media, and incidents are either the product of the author's imagination or are used fictitiously. The author acknowledges the trademark status and ownership of any location names or products mentioned in this book. The author received no compensation for any mention of said trademark.

No part of this book may be reproduced in any form or by any electronic or mechanical means, including information storage and retrieval systems, without written permission from the author, except for the use of brief quotations in a book review.

Cover Model: Travis Norwood
Photographer: Tonya Clark
Graphic Designer: Irene Johnson
Editor: Katrina Fair

Chapter 1

Ashley

"Another voicemail. I wish he'd get a clue and leave me alone."

"Maybe if you didn't fuck him the night you met him," my best friend, Raye, always so helpful. "Look, Ashley, I don't know why you're fighting it. It's obvious you're into him. I can only think of one other time in the twenty-eight years I've known you that you went for it on the first date. Shit, and we've both known Dominic since grade school—he doesn't even count."

I cringe at the memory of my drunk night with Dom. My reminder that, just because you've known the guy forever, it doesn't mean it's safe to get drunk with him. He's still a guy and he'll still fuck you if he gets the chance. "Everybody makes mistakes. Dom and Jonah were both mistakes."

"You weren't drunk when you did Jonah," she glares at me as a dirty smile crosses her lips.

"Women have needs," I state matter-of-factly.

"And you needed Jonah?"

"Don't play coy with me. You would've done him if you saw him first."

"What's your point? We all know I'm a ho," Raye shruggs.

I gaze off into the ocean, remembering the night with Jonah while I sit at an oceanside cafe having lunch with my bestie. I hear her muttering on about something, but she's drowned out by my heated memories. My hands exploring his rock hard abs, tracing each with my fingers and then my tongue, kissing every single one of them before I moved onto the next. His fingers threading through my long auburn hair, guiding my mouth to his. His hard body beneath me when he claims my mouth with caveman-like desire, unexpected from his professional attire and demeanor. He controlled me with my hair wrapped around his wrist, using it to hold me where he wanted me and didn't allow me to break the kiss that pulled me into him. The kiss that was the end of me. The kiss that would make me his. The kiss that made me do stupid things. The kiss that can never happen again. He sat up and pulled me into his lap, kissing me the whole time and not letting me go. The tension from my hair, amazing, making it hotter. His words, "Okay, Ashley?" were soft and warm at my ear. I responded with a nod, overcome by the sensation of his hands on me. His lips, sealed to mine, he shoves his hard cock up into me and kisses me deeper. He pulls my head back and gazes into my eyes. I can't control myself as I move on him. He pulled my hair harder, bared my neck to him and nibbled at my collarbone until I started to moan. He chuckled as he lifted me and fucked me against the wall of his bedroom...

"Hello! Are you listening to me?"

Raye startles me back into reality, but I play it off, "Of course, you're talking about that guy."

She rolls her eyes at me, "You aren't fooling me. You know you want him. Call him back."

I wave her on and change the conversation because I don't want to talk about it. I've already spent too many nights imagining his warm chestnut eyes searching mine while he made love to me.

Chapter 2

Jonah

Why the fuck won't she answer her phone? I told her I'd be back when I left. "Ashley, it's not funny anymore. Answer my calls. I know it's been a few weeks. I'm sorry. I can't control my work schedule. You know I'm close to getting what I want here. Please call me." Leaving her messages is the only thing I've been able to do for the last few weeks. I thought it was going well. She rocks my world in and out of bed. We're so compatible it's stupid. She answered the phone for the first week I was gone and the conversations we had were thoughtful, real, and felt like we had a future, but since then it's been radio silence. I'm not sure what happened. My guess is that I didn't go back when she expected me. I hate not being in control, but I'm in line to take over as CEO and I can't show any weakness. I have to be perfect or they will skip over me like I don't even exist. One chink in my armor is all it takes. I want the experience so I can start my own business, but mostly I'm after the annual seven-figure bonus to fund it. Only two or three years of working like hell wherever I need to be to keep the business in line and growing profitably and I'll be set. Long hours bouncing between the New York, Chicago, and Dallas offices make it difficult. I'm too far away to go get her and fucked up by the time difference. The Orange County beaches of Southern California, where I found her, are a world away.

Chapter 3

Ashley

"I really don't understand you. Why are you home watching old movies with me on a Saturday night, when you could be hooking up with the hottie who keeps leaving you messages?" Raye rattles with her mouth full of popcorn.

"Why are you home watching old movies with me?" I sneer at her.

"Everyone knows us hos don't go out until after midnight. You have to keep the dogs waiting. Swoop in like the eye-candy I am after they've already taken stock of everyone else and wait for them to crowd around me." She stops to check the time on her phone. "You've only got me for a few hours, then I've got to sparkle up for the club."

"Go make some more popcorn 'sparkle' since you ate it all, and make it the good way."

"Yea, yea, yea... I know, more sea salt, fresh cracked black pepper, and cheese powder."

"And don't burn it this time. Don't use that dayglo orange cheese powder this time, it's nasty. There's some parmesan in the fridge."

"You can do it yourself if you're going to be picky," she chuckles using a smart-ass tone.

"Can't you see I'm busy picking our movies for the evening? No appreciation for my movie theme skills at all."

There's a loud unexpected knock on the door and Raye jumps at the noise, immediately re-routing her kitchen trip to the front door. She peeks through the peephole, "Ummm, Ashley?"

"What?"

"Are you expecting a hottie? Did you start answering his calls and not tell me?" She opens the door before I can respond, "Hi, Jonah, come on in!"

"Hey, sorry to stop by without calling, but I figured you wouldn't answer anyway," he says with a weak grin.

I can smell him from across the room. His cologne is amazing. It must have pheromones or something. I need to find the antidote, but I'm afraid it's already too late for me tonight. Damn it! I want him.

"Well, I'm going to excuse myself and leave you two to fornicate in private," Raye mumbles as she walks to the other side of the house where her room is.

He's focused on me and standing at the door, "Am I allowed to come in?"

"Sure, but stay on that side of the room."

"I want to be on your side of the room," he closes the door behind him, securely latching the lock.

Great, he locked himself in with me and he's what I need to be protected from.

"What are you doing here?" I ask timidly and wonder why it came out that way.

He gazes into my eyes with the warmth I remember, "I just flew in from Dallas because it's the first opportunity I've had with time to see you." He sits down next to me and rests his hand on my knee. "Why wouldn't you answer my calls?"

"I don't want to be a distraction for you. You don't have time for me."

"I found time for you," he gazes into my eyes and I can't stop him. I don't want to stop him. He kisses me. That kiss again. It's all it takes and I'm his.

Chapter 4

Jonah

I've wondered for weeks if I was remembering her correctly or if I'd lost my mind. Her lips are full and soft. She tastes like sweet ripe strawberries and I want to eat her up. I lean into her ear and slide my hands down to her hips. I can't help myself as I inhale her scent and nibble at her ear. The curve of her hips, the way she reacts to me. I'm overcome by the memories of being with her and I need her, want her again. I didn't think it was real. One woman couldn't make me want only her. It had to be one of those *you always want what you can't have scenarios*. But now that I'm here and have her in my arms, taste her on my lips—It's the one thing I don't have a plan for. Ashley's more than the vivid memories I've been playing in my head. I need to find a way to keep her beyond tonight, even if tonight is all of the time I have.

Naomi Springthorp

I'VE GOT TO LEAVE. The corporate jet is scheduled to take off in less than an hour. Fuck, 5am is early. I don't want to leave her again. I can't go weeks without her. I'll be back sooner. I'll call her everyday. I'll get her to come to me. Damn it! She's finally sleeping. I kept her up all night. I shouldn't wake her.

Chapter 5

Ashley

When I have hours of hot as fuck sex with Jonah and fall asleep satisfied in his arms, he should still be here when I wake up. Stop jumping to conclusions, Ashley. We got this. He wouldn't leave without saying anything, especially after last night. "Jonah?" I call out for him, confident that he's here and hear the front door latch.

Raye walks into my bedroom wearing her club clothes from last night and leans in the doorway, swiveling her head around like she's missing something or might be buzzing. "Jonah?" she yells. "I don't think he's here."

"It's not supposed to be like this. This is not how this goes. He can't keep popping in to see me whenever he wants and then disappearing!" I rant giving away more info than I have in the past and definitely more than I intended.

"Hold up there, exactly how many nights have you spent with the hottie?" She stops and observes me, then in a calmer tone, "Let me try that again. Remember you will always be my sister from another mister and I will have your back until the end. You want to talk?"

I can't hide the tears welling up in my eyes. One single word out of my mouth will turn to full-on bawling. I'm stuck needing to talk and I can't speak without showing my weakness.

"It will always be chicks before dicks with us. But if he's the dick you want, make it happen. I'll help you."

The tears stream silently down my cheeks as I laugh at her honest sincerity. I reach over to my nightstand and grab my phone to see:

Jonah: I didn't want to leave you.
Jonah: I didn't have a choice.
Jonah: You'd just fallen asleep and I decided not to wake you.
Jonah: I know it would've been better if I were still there.
Jonah: I want to still be there.
Jonah: Please don't shut me out again.
Jonah: Make my day and call me when you wake up.

"What the fuck? Why are you smiling like a fool?" Raye shakes her head and walks toward me, trying to read my texts over my shoulder. "That has you smiling?" She turns to walk away and stops dead in her tracks, spinning back toward me on her heel, "You're in love with this guy."

"No way."

"Try again," she says and glares at me.

"Maybe I'm attached, a little. I'm sure it's the sex thing."

"Spill."

I feel my own eyes roll as the words pour out, "It was at least twice a week, usually more for the first couple months. Then only texts and phone calls for the last seven weeks. I quit answering him three weeks ago. He doesn't have time for me. I get it. He's busy. It's not enough for me, so I let him go."

"How did I miss him here that much?"

"It wasn't always here. Sometimes when you were at work, and it was during your 'Maddux Phase,'" I state as if she'd been addicted to the newest pop music star.

"Hmmm, about that, I ran into Maddux last night at the club."

"Are we going to re-live the 'Maddux Phase'?"

She puts her hand on her hip, "Do you know how hard it is to find a man like that? He's a true sugar daddy, none of that splenda shit. Plus, his peen is above average and he knows how to use it."

"Jonah uses his tongue and then his peen."

"Bitch."

Chapter 6

Ashley

Has he forgotten me again? It's obvious he's already taken me for granted. I mean seriously! I shut him out before and I should've stuck to it. I know better. Men never change. They are who they are. Once a jerk, always a jerk. I admit he was very attentive and apologetic for the couple weeks after he came to find me and fucked me all night long. He knows I can walk away. That night together was something special. Listen to me, something special. Forget him. He's just another guy. It's time to move on. I argue with myself as I go through my mail until I find an express overnight envelope from Jonah and rip it open. My cheeks warm and there's an involuntary smile on my lips when I read the note inside:

Ashley,

I should've been back to see you multiple times by now and I can't figure out how to manage it with my schedule, so I thought maybe you'd visit me. I'll be working in New York later this week. I've got a couple of short days and two full days off for the weekend, which never happens. I'd love to show you the city and spend some time with you. I want to be with you. I miss you and it's more than your sexy ass. Check the itinerary on the plane tickets attached and let me know. I can change them to whatever works best for you. I want you here.

Yours,
Jonah

It's an open-ended first class ticket scheduled to fly non-stop to JFK on Thursday morning. That's four days from now. I've always wanted to go to New York. I can't jump that quickly. I've got business too. Maybe. It's only a long weekend.

> To Jonah: Hypothetically, where will I be staying in New York?
> Jonah: With me.
> To Jonah: How will I know where to go when I get off the plane?
> Jonah: My driver will pick you up.

Driver?

To Jonah: Where will your driver be taking me?
Jonah: Fifth Ave and E 64th St.

I quickly search the intersection on my phone. It's on Central Park! Fuck! I've always wanted to go there. This is not helping my willpower. I need to cut him loose and stop thinking about him, waiting for him... missing him. He's not what I want. Okay, he is what I want. But, it doesn't matter. The timing isn't right. I'm ready for him now and he needs a few years. I'm not going to put my life on hold for any man. He can take the chance and check back with me when he's ready. No telling where I'll be in life then. He might get lucky, or maybe we might get lucky.

My phone rings, "Hello?"

"So, what do you say? Come to me in New York, beautiful," his silky tone caresses my ear.

"I'm sorry, who's this?"

"Don't play with me, Ashley."

"Interesting, how do you know my name?"

"I get it. It's been too long. I promise to make it up to you."

"How?"

"Pleasuring you all night and being there when you wake up."

"Go on."

"I'll make you breakfast in bed."

"Uh huh."

"I'll take you to a show on Broadway."

"Is that all?"

"A carriage ride around Central Park and dinner at Tavern on the Green."

"Hhhmmm..."

"Anything you want. Just come to me and let me show you how much you mean to me. Please, Ashley."

"How much do I mean to you?"

"There's nobody, but you."

"Four days isn't much notice. I have business to handle, too."

"Tell me when and I'll change it. I thought you might like to visit New York and it's rare that I get a weekend off here."

"I'll let you know tomorrow. I want to see you," I hang up before he can say anymore.

"Who do you want to see?" I turn to see Raye standing in the middle of the room.

"Nobody."

"It sounds like you're going somewhere this weekend."

"New York," I'm beaming and I'm going no matter what.

"You look like a girl who's getting laid this weekend," she high-fives me as she goes on about her business.

Chapter 7

Jonah

All day I've been hearing her voice in my head. It's not enough. I dial her number and listen to it ring, wondering if she'll answer.

"Hello?"

"Hi, beautiful. I'm looking forward to you. Been thinking about you all day."

"I'm not sure I should be visiting you, but I'm going to. I like the phone calls today."

"If the calls make you that happy, there will be calls every day from now on. I guarantee it."

"Guarantee? I'll believe it when it happens."

"No faith in me?"

"You don't have the best track record."

"I suppose that's true. I'm trying to do better."

Chapter 8

Ashley

I wake up Tuesday morning grumpy and curse at myself for having a menstrual cycle with a mind of its own. All the signs are there, everything from being irritable and bloated to sore breasts and an achy back. I'll be starting soon. This is horrible timing. I'm going to see Jonah this weekend and one of the things I'm planning on seeing in New York is his bedroom. Maybe I can ignore it and it'll go away.

I manage to get my work caught up, though I did have a couple of long phone calls. It's hard to cut calls short when all of the people you work with are family. My family owns property across North America, and it's something that's stayed in the family. The property never gets sold, simply rented, rehabbed, and repeat until it gets passed to the next family member. Essentially, I'm the property manager. My great-grandmother left me the house I live in and an apartment building—mortgage free. I've purchased a few duplexes and my parents will be leaving their property to me with the catch that I have to give my brother part of the rent money for doing absolutely nothing each month. He's horrible with money and he'd be the first in the family to sell a piece of property. Most likely to buy a new video game system and possibly a third motorcycle, or a sports car, and then hit the strip club with whatever he had left. Leo is the baby and has always been treated like one. He'll never work a day in his life. I prefer to be involved and work with the property. I wasn't meant to be born into money and I need to do my part. I've been told I can pass the management responsibilities on to one of my cousins, but I've got it streamlined and honestly it doesn't take that much effort for me. Besides, I like to know things are getting done right. I've been told I'm a control freak. If that means things get done correctly, then I suppose I am.

Tonight my goal is laundry and packing, so tomorrow I can spend the day primping. There's no way I'm going to New York without a fresh manicure and I'd like to glow when he sees me, so maybe a facial and some other personal spoiling is in order. A day at the spa sounds wonderful.

My phone rings and I grin from ear to ear when I check the caller ID, "Hello?"

"Hi beautiful," Jonah's voice warms me through the phone.

"Beautiful? Are you sure you've got the right person? Oh, I get it, that's what you call all of your women to keep from getting a name wrong."

He releases an annoyed chuckle, "When I call you beautiful, I'm remembering you. Your long thick auburn hair, silky as I run my fingers through it, wanting to grasp it and use it to hold you against me. Your clear green eyes piercing my heart with every glance my direction, as if you can read my soul. The delicate structure of your cheekbones, smooth when I caress your face and trace your lips with my fingers. Your lips so sweet and full when I kiss you, driving me to need all of you. Your breathless voice when you declare my name and give yourself to me. Your feminine shape in my hands while I worship you."

My sharp tongue is silenced by his words.

"Ashley?" He stops, waiting for a response. "Ashley? I can hear you breathing."

"I want you, too," slips quietly from my lips.

"If you want me, why were you ignoring me?"

"Ignoring you is easier than admitting I have emotions. You disappear."

"There's only you. The only thing in the way is work."

"I know how important your job is to you. We talked about this months ago. It's your path to your goals. It's how you earn the money you need for your dreams."

"I have other dreams."

"You're dirty. You know what I meant."

"I do. I can have both."

"It's not what I've seen. You work and forget about me until you can squeeze in a few minutes, then you disappear again."

"Ashe, you are so much more. I'm sorry I haven't been able to show you. I promise to make it up to you this weekend."

"A weekend isn't enough."

"Then this weekend will be our new start. Give me a chance to prove how much you mean to me. Yes, it might be weekends for a few years, but after that I'll be able to give you everything. It'll be worth the wait. I promise."

I don't need him the way he thinks I do. I don't want for anything material. "More promises." Promises I don't need. I want his love, not his money.

"Don't be like that. Fly to New York."

"Jonah," Words spew out of my mouth, "I can't tell you

no. I want to be with you." Shocking myself with my words, I gasp for air as I realize I'm in love with him.

"Are you okay?"

"Yes. Ummm, no. Goodnight." I hang up and crawl into bed.

> Jonah: Tell me what's wrong.
> To Jonah: My heart doesn't get to control my mouth.
> To Jonah: Goodnight.

Wednesday I wake up sick to my stomach. I toss everything, my cookies included. My head hurts from crying in the night and I'm upset with myself for not controlling my tongue. I've never known how to control my heart, but I've always been able to walk away from men. I have so much to do before I can leave, yet all I want to do is sleep.

Chapter 9

Jonah

I've called her three times and she isn't answering. I've left messages and she isn't returning my call. She's supposed to be here in less than 24 hours and I haven't so much as gotten a text from her. This is all too familiar.

> To Ashley: I've been calling and you're not answering.
> To Ashley: It's getting late.
> To Ashley: Please tell me you're busy packing.
> To Ashley: This feels like when you are ignoring me.

She said she wants to be with me. What's she doing?

It's getting late and I've got an early morning. I'm trying one more time...

"Hello?"

"Ashe?" It doesn't sound like her.

"Yeah."

"Are you okay?"

"Yeah, mmmm sleep."

"Are you ready to come to me tomorrow?"

"I could come for you now."

Uh, hmm. "What do you mean?"

"I love it when you make me come."

"Yeah?"

"Uh-huh. Especially the part with your tongue."

I can't. She's asleep. Can I? "You mean kissing you with my tongue?"

"Uh-huh, down there."

I can hear her squirming in between the sheets. She's killing me. All I want to do is make her sweet body come for me. "If I was there, I'd be holding you close to me with my arms wrapped around you. Close enough to feel your breath on my skin and smell your coconut scented hair. Our legs entangled tightly, your heat against my thigh and my hard cock dragging across your body. I kiss your lips tenderly, taking special care and paying attention to every part of your lips before sliding my tongue into your mouth to tangle with yours. Your whole body reacts to me. I run my fingers through your long hair and tease your breasts while I continue to kiss you. Slowly, I move my hands down your belly and caress your thighs as I lift your legs up into the air. I slide your panties off and stop to admire your feminine curves. I move down on the bed, leaving a line of kisses on your belly as I make my way to your heaven. You smell so sweet that I can't help myself and dive right into your hot wet pussy. Licking your seam up one side and down the other repeatedly. Stopping at the top to find your clit and settle in with your pleasure in mind. I lightly lick and suck at your clit while I push a finger into your wet entrance. Stroking you with my finger, I add a second finger and keep licking your center. I pull my fingers out and rub your clit as I French kiss your pussy. Pressing my mouth to your heat and rubbing my nose in your seam." She's making happy noises, "Ashe, are you touching yourself?"

"Huh?" She's still asleep, "Maybe."

That means yes. She'll deny it tomorrow. "I'm licking you in the spot you like. Over and over, and I won't stop until you come for me. I might not stop then. All I want to do is pleasure you, beautiful. Feel me touching you? Licking you? Kissing you? Sucking on you?"

She cries out.

"Yes, beautiful. I'm not stopping. Come for me." Fuck me. I'm so fucking hard. Her noises are driving me insane. I need her so bad.

"Jonah! Mmmmm." About a minute passes, "Hello?"

"I'm here."

"Who is this?"

"You're Ashley and I'm Jonah," I answer laughing.

"Why are you on the phone?"

"I called. You answered and told me to make you come."

"Huh, I guess you can follow directions. Goodnight." She hangs up on me without another word.

Chapter 10

Ashley

Thursday morning I wake up earlier than planned in the middle of a dream. Dreaming of my arms wrapped protectively around my belly, relaxing on the beach wearing a big floppy hat and sunglasses large enough to cover my entire face. Vivid visions of a newborn baby in my arms. Flashes of a young toddler playing in the surf's edge at the beach. I wake having to puke and I wonder, could I be...?

It's not the first time I've wondered. I have a test stashed in my bathroom. I dig it out and pee on the stick. I leave it to sit for a few minutes and try to ignore that I might be pregnant while I gnaw on some crackers and try not to blow chunks again. I know I'm not. This is silly. It was only a dream. I'm obviously sick. The illness is probably giving me weird dreams. I check the test and see two lines. Doesn't two lines mean... Where's the instructions? I read through the instructions. I followed the correct procedure. Everything is accurate. Two lines is positive. Positive? Huh, sounds like an opinion not a result. I'm pregnant.

I find myself standing in the shower with the water

falling over me. The warmth of the spray calming me and reminding me of the huge soft drops of rain in Hawaii. I immediately pack my bikinis, my favorite beach clothes, and a variety of everything else. I grab my work bag from the closet with my laptop and accessories. I slide my sunglasses onto my head of wet hair and slip into my flip-flops.

I get to the airport and trade my ticket to New York in for a flight to Hawaii. I get lucky and take the last seat on the next flight out to Oahu. I can't go to New York. Eventually he'll come looking for me, I can't be here for him to find me. He doesn't have time for me. There's no way he has time for a child. It's better if he doesn't know. He can forget about me and work toward his dream. I want him to achieve his goals. I want him to be happy. I don't need him. I can do this on my own. Everything will be fine.

I land in Honolulu and call Raye, "I landed."

"How was your flight? I was expecting to hear from you already."

"I changed it."

"You changed it?"

"Yep."

"Care to elaborate?"

"Not really."

"You know the rules. We may not tell anyone else, but we always know where each other are. So, where are you?"

"Hawaii."

"Why? What happened to getting laid this weekend? Oh! Is hottie meeting you in Hawaii?"

"No, he doesn't know and we aren't going to tell him."

"Okay. When are you coming back?"

"I'm going to do inspections of the properties here and see how it goes. Maybe stay awhile."

"This may be the first time in twenty-eight years that

you've acted like someone with a trust fund. I'm not used to it. It's about time you did something for you. Why now?"

"It's better if I don't hook up with Jonah. I'm turning this into a work trip."

"I'll be here watching our house. Have fun. Feel free to send me a plane ticket so I can visit," she laughs.

"Don't tell him where I am. I'll check in soon." I hang up and walk through the airport, stopping to pick up a big floppy hat and red sarong on my way to the rental car counter. If I'm acting like the trust fund baby, I might as well do it right. I rent the convertible Audi A5 Cabriolet and load my luggage into the backseat with the top down. I use the sarong like a scarf and tie my hat on. I push my sunglasses up my nose and take off alone for the North Shore Shacks property. They're not shacks. It's a variety of small vacation rentals, ranging from studios to two-bedroom beach houses. My family keeps the upstairs two-bedroom for family use only and I'm going to move in for a few weeks. I'm the property manager, so I'm aware of the vacancies and luckily no family is visiting Hawaii right now. The onsite maintenance crew keeps everything clean, Auntie Kala oversees it all and makes sure of it.

I park at the shacks and wander the property until I get to the beach, enjoying the warm sand between my toes and the mist from the ocean on my face. I turn to face the property and see people on the balcony at our family unit.

Walking toward the unit I meet up with Auntie, "Ashley! I didn't know you were visiting! It's been so long since I've seen you!" She wraps her arms around me and squeezes.

"It was kind of a last minute decision. I forgot how beautiful it is here. I'm thinking I might stay for awhile."

"Perfect! It will be nice to have you around."

"Is the family unit occupied?"

"Oh! I can get them out. No worries."

"Who's staying there?"

"My nephew lives on the Big Island and his job got transferred here. He's been commuting and staying with me during the week, but his wife is pregnant and they already have three kids. Too much for her to do alone, so I brought them here so I can help. My house is too small." She laughs, "And, I need a break from them, too."

"Are any of the shacks available?"

"Yes. Good idea. I can move them there temporarily."

"No, I'll take the shack. I don't need much room."

"Are you sure?" Auntie asks wide-eyed.

"Yea. It'll be a nice change. Quiet and cozy."

"Then let me give it a quick cleaning and send one of the kids to help you with your luggage. You're welcome to join us for dinner."

"Thank you. Don't take it personal, I need some alone time."

Kala cocks her head and examines me, "I'm here when you need me." She turns to walk away, and yells back at me, "How long are you staying?"

"I don't know yet. A few weeks. Maybe months."

Auntie stops in her tracks surprised by my response, "Okay. Always here for you."

I walk to the water and let the surf reach my toes, standing in the same place and allowing the waves to pull the sand from under my feet. I find a warm patch of white sand that's just out of reach from the ocean and sit cross-legged watching the waves roll in and pound the shore. Quietly relaxing and absorbing my surroundings. What am I doing here?

I'm startled by my phone ringing and check to see who's calling. Jonah. Of course, he's expecting me, I'm not there, and I'm not going to be. I don't answer.

Jonah: Where are you?
To Jonah: Decided not to visit New York.
Jonah: What happened?
Jonah: You wanted to be with me last night. What changed your mind?
To Jonah: Forget me. It's better that way.
Jonah: No
Jonah: Ashley!
Jonah: Please don't shut me out.

Tears stream down my cheeks, but I can't be the reason he doesn't get his dream. I bury my face in the palms of my hands and cry until dark. Auntie finds me and helps me to my shack without words. She leaves me a warm homemade meal, fresh pineapple, and water. My bed is already turned down and I crawl into it, unable to handle anything else today.

I wake the next morning ready to throw up again and Auntie catches me praying to the toilet bowl gods.

"Are you okay?"

"Yes. Must've caught something on the plane."

"Try again or are you in denial?"

"Denial."

"You here to hide for nine months?"

"Thinking about it."

"Your secret is safe with me. I'll help you. Everything will be fine. Happy mommy to be and happy baby staying here."

"Thank you, Kala."

I get dressed and drive the two blocks to the market. I purchase snacks, two more tests, crackers, ginger ale, and a plate lunch. I realize I'm pregnant, I want to make triple sure before I make anymore decisions.

Chapter 11

Jonah

I can't believe she ditched me and shut me out. It was always a possibility. She has shut me out before. I don't like it, but I can fix it.

> To Ashley: Can we talk?
> To Ashley: Please. Beautiful?
> To Ashley: I don't understand. I thought you wanted to see me too.
> To Ashley: I thought you were excited to visit New York.

I wait a few hours and get no response.

> To Ashley: At least acknowledge that you see my texts.

As I'm falling asleep, I want to hear her voice and wonder if...

> To Ashley: You know we're more than sex, right?

Naomi Springthorp

I need to go to her and show up at her place and everything will be fine. This woman makes me crazy. I've never even considered chasing anyone until her and it's the worst possible time for the distraction. I'm so close to getting the CEO position. It's down to two of us and I've been told I'm the front-runner.

There must be a way to get the girl and the job. I'm stuck in New York for a few more days. Maybe I should send some New York to her.

Chapter 12

Ashley

I walk into my shack and my texts light up. There must not be good service out on the beach. Another reason to spend more time relaxing on the sand. I question if it's truly more than sex on his end, but my heart believes it. Honestly, it's why I'm here. I love him and want him to have everything he desires. A pregnant woman would simply be in his way. I need to end this for his own good. He doesn't need to be thinking about me.

> To Jonah: I'm fine.
> To Jonah: No need to text me.
> To Jonah: Goodbye.

Tears stream down my face and my hand is on my belly, "It's better for him this way."

Chapter 13

Jonah

Goodbye? No fucking way! I call her.

"Hello?" She answers sleepily.

Shit! I hate time zones. "This isn't goodbye. This is our beginning. Stop trying to shut me out, Ashley."

"What? I'm sleeping. Why are you calling me in the middle of the night?"

"You don't respond during the day. At least I know you are still breathing."

"I don't respond because I don't want to talk to you. We're done! It's over!" She hangs up, but I swear I could hear her crying.

I don't understand what's going on, but I'm not giving up. This has to stop now.

I call my assistant, "Jonah Price's office."

"Hey Mighty Midge, is there any way I can disappear for 24 hours and use the corporate jet?"

"Where are you going? When do you want to go?"

"I need to make a visit to Southern California as soon as possible."

"Let me review the calendar and I'll text options shortly." She hangs up. Pint sized, all business, loyal, and the best assistant in the clerical pool.

Before I can leave for the office...

Midge - The jet is only available for 12 hours today.
Midge - Can you wait a couple days? I can cover everything on your schedule during that time and you can disappear for 36 hours easily with the jet.

I want to go now, but she's always right. Ashley will be more receptive if I have more time. I can't leave her sleeping again.

To Midge - A couple days will be fine. Please make that happen.
Midge - Consider it done.

I LAND in Orange County and immediately take an Uber to her house. Walking up to the door it's quiet and lifeless. I knock and ring the doorbell. Nothing. I leave my business card on the door with a note written on the back:

Ashley,

I'm here for 36 hours. I want to see you. I need to see you. We're not done. Please call me.

Jonah

Naomi Springthorp

I walk a couple of blocks to the nearest hotel and check-in, hoping she'll call me. I walk back to her place repeatedly to catch her when she gets home, but it's always quiet with no lights coming on even into the evening.

> To Ashley: I'm at the hotel near your place.
> To Ashley: I've been to your house.
> To Ashley: Where are you?

Nothing. No response and no sign of anyone being home.

Chapter 14

Ashley

Every day gets easier and harder at the same time. I've been on the North Shore long enough to form a new daily routine and I'm pregnant enough to learn that routines are meant to be flexible. Well, I've created a pretty relaxed routine and Auntie Kala spoils me.

It's been easier since I got the morning sickness under control. I swear pineapple is magic. The locals all say it fixes things, all kinds of things, things you can't even imagine. The one thing I know it does, help an unsettled stomach. I know, strange. Add the ginger candies Auntie has been bringing me, with the fresh pineapple she makes sure I always have available, and bye-bye morning sickness.

I've been handling all of my work email and calls in the morning. The time difference in Hawaii makes it too late to call the mainland in the afternoon and I'm fine with that. I'd rather get it done and relax. Kala checks in on me every morning and has taken it upon herself to provide meals for me. She wants to make sure I'm eating right and not overexerting. She keeps reminding me to drink fluids, eat pineapple, and keep shade available when I'm out in the sun.

I've been spending my days on the beach in a bikini. Yes, even with my obviously pregnant belly. It's just me in my huge floppy hat and a beach towel. I've been wandering off to do inspections of my families other properties and stopping at the local swap meets to shop for clothes. They have Hawaiian print everything. I bought a bikini and a sundress and mailed it to Raye. Mostly, it's been sundresses and bikinis for me too, but the bikinis are because mine have gotten too small and the full-cut sundresses are comfortable. Raye would hate them, but she'll love the dress I sent her. I could see it accentuating her assets on first sight and she simply needed to have it.

I don't make it very late into the evening before I pass out. I'm always tired. Luckily, I have help and most of my work requires me to sit, type, and talk. I never saw myself as someone that kept to herself, but this experience is teaching me things.

Time for my weekly call to check in with Raye and my phone rings like clockwork, "Hey!"

"Hey you! Since I got a package does that mean you're done working there, have time to spare, and ready to come home?"

"Not yet. Did you try on that dress? That hot pink floral print is going to look amazing on you."

"Yes, and of course it does. It's in line and waiting for the next beach party. Thank you. Am I supposed to wear the matching skimpy bikini underneath it?"

"Duh, I can't have my girl out without the matching set."

"So, the gift is an offering to buy you more time away because you know you should be home by now?"

Shit. "I saw it and thought of you. You needed to have it."

"Uh huh. When are you coming home?"

"Not sure yet."

"Do you have a guy over there that you're hiding from me?" Her attitude is shining.

In a way, yes. But, Raye isn't talking about the baby boy I haven't told her about yet. "No." I laugh, "Unless you count the bellman that brings me my room service."

"What kind of service does he provide? If his tongue or cock are involved, then he counts." She stops, "You have a package I hesitate to tell you about."

"What package? I'm not expecting anything."

"It's from the reason you're there. I don't know what he did to you, but I almost wish you were shagging the bellman to get over him."

"Open it."

She takes a minute to get the box open and it sounds like she pulls something out of the box, "It's a basket full of New York."

"Like manhole covers and taxis or what? Details please."

"Animal crackers and a T-Shirt from Central Park Zoo, a bag of gourmet candies from Chelsea Market, a metal taxi filled with taffy, a Statue of Liberty magnet, and an I heart NY tote bag. Hold on, I think there's something else in the bottom."

"What?"

"Ashe, it's a Tiffany bag."

I listen as she pulls it from the package.

"I'm going to text you photos. I swear the Tiffany's packaging is worth buying something there."

I hope he didn't spend a lot of money on me. "So, what is it?"

Raye releases a sigh, "It's the silver charm bracelet with the heart shaped return to Tiffany's charm on it."

I've always wanted one of those, but it's the kind of thing that you don't buy for yourself. Someone buys it for you and then they buy you charms for gifts. "No card?"

"Still digging to the bottom. Yes, a notecard in an envelope. Opening it now. It says:

Ashley,

Since you didn't make it to New York, I thought I'd send a little bit of New York to you. I wish you would stop shutting me out. At the least, tell me what I did wrong and I will fix it.

Please call me.

Jonah

"What did he do wrong? Didn't he dump you or something? I don't really understand why you went to Hawaii instead of New York."

"He can't keep popping into my life whenever it suits him. I couldn't put myself through a weekend with him just to be forgotten again until he found time."

"So, you ran away and shut him out?"

"Yep."

"Seems a bit extreme."

"Who's side are you on here?"

"It's always chicks before dicks, but he's the dick you want and this doesn't make any sense."

"Thanks for understanding," I hang up agitated and feel a kick for the first time. I want to tell her about my Mac Nut, but then she'd tell everybody and probably show up here. I don't want to deal with it. I want to be alone.

Chapter 15

Jonah

To Ashley: Hi.
To Ashley: Can we talk?
Ashley: Please leave me alone.
Ashley: I told you it's over.
To Ashley: It's not over. I need to understand.
Ashley: Can't explain.
To Ashley: Just tell me what I did or didn't do.
To Ashley: I was trying and you didn't let me make it up to you.
To Ashley: I promise it would be different.
To Ashley: I promise I'd call you every day at the very least.
Ashley: Please leave me alone.

I need another angle. I'm going back to try her house again. A few days later I'm back at her front door and it isn't as lifeless. There are lights on inside and music paying. I knock on the door and wait. I knock again and still nothing. I ring the doorbell. The music stops and I swear I can hear someone on the other side of the door. But the door doesn't open and the music gets turned back up, louder than it was before. I bang on the door, "Please open the door." Nothing.

I do the same thing every few hours and there's obviously someone home.

> To Ashley: The least you could do is open the door.
> To Ashley: I know your home.
> To Ashley: I heard you turn the music up.
> Ashley: Sorry, I'm not home. You can't just find me and kiss me and have me.
> To Ashley: That's not what I want. I want you.

It may not be Ashley, but somebody's home. I need a new tactic. I write a note:

I need to see Ashley. I don't know what happened. Please help me. Call me.

I left my number. If she's not here, I need to know where she is. I go to my room for the night and send a text.

> To Ashley: You make me crazy.
> To Ashley: You are special like no other woman.
> To Ashley: Please think about talking to me.
> Unknown: Ashley isn't here.
> To Unknown: When will she be back?
> Unknown: She won't tell me. She said she was going to New York and went somewhere else.
> To Unknown: She's been gone that long?
> Unknown: Yes.
> To Unknown: I need to find her.
> Unknown: Sorry.

Why is she staying away for so long? She has work obligations, too.

> To Ashley: I'm thinking about you.
> To Ashley: I wish you would talk to me.
> To Ashley: I'm not giving up.
> Ashley: Make it easier on both of us and walk away.
> To Ashley: I'm not going away.
> To Ashley: Give me a chance.
> Ashley: I wish you would listen to me and understand.
> To Ashley: Call me and I'll listen.
> To Ashley: Answer my calls and I'll listen.

WHEN SHE RESPONDS to me it tells me I still have a chance. As minimal as her responses are it gives me hope and spurs me on to find another way. Maybe I can get to her through the roommate.

> To Unknown: Can you help me?
> Unknown: Chicks before dicks.
> To Unknown: I understand that. I don't want you to give anything away.
> Unknown: ?
> To Unknown: Why did she change her mind and not fly to visit me in New York?
> Unknown: I thought you dumped her until a few weeks ago.
> To Unknown: I didn't dump her. I've been texting her or calling her everyday.

Naomi Springthorp

Unknown: She's staying away from you.
Unknown: She won't tell me when she's coming back.
To Unknown: I'm aware that I didn't pay enough attention to her, that I was gone for too long, and she feels like I don't have time for her.
To Unknown: The New York trip was the first step in making up for that and proving to her she's the only one.
Unknown: Men are dogs. She's not the only one.
To Unknown: She's been the only one since I met her.
To Unknown: Nobody compares to her.

Chapter 16

Ashley

A child wasn't on my immediate agenda. Maybe in the future after I met 'the one' and got married. Maybe after we had an amazing honeymoon and settled into our own place together. Maybe then it could be a possibility. My family is proper and I'm the level-headed one of my generation. Not the one who would run away to deal with a pregnancy alone. It's true. I'm hiding it like I did something bad. Auntie Kala is the only one who knows. I haven't told my mother or anyone else. Personally, I'm embracing the situation and growing happier every day with my Mac Nut. Though he's bigger than a nut at this point and kicks like a soccer player who thinks my bladder is the ball.

As I lay on the beach relaxing with the breeze from the ocean blowing over my skin, I watch the beach goers. Some swim out on their surfboard and wait for the perfect wave. Others lie in the sun, flipping over every fifteen minutes to get a tropical tan. Kids build sandcastles and play in the water as it climbs up onto the shore. I wonder if my Mac Nut will be one of those kids or grow up to be one of those surfers.

I'm startled by my phone ringing and realize it's time for my call from Raye, "Hey!" I love talking to her. She's my connection to the real world, or maybe my old world.

"When are you coming home?"

What the heck? "Yes, I'm having a great day. Thanks for asking," I respond to what she should've asked.

"I'm glad to hear it. Mine is fair. My bestie ditched me months ago and won't tell me when she's coming home. The guy who I thought had dumped her and broke her has been coming by the house looking for her and leaving notes and texting me trying to find her."

"How did he get your number?"

"He left a note under the door saying he needed to find you and please call. I sent him a text, but didn't tell him who I am. Don't worry, I didn't tell him where you are."

"Why'd you respond to him?" Irritated that my bestie engaged.

"Because I don't know what to do anymore. You aren't making any sense. He didn't dump you. You ran away. You are acting like a fucking trust fund baby. There's something going on and it's not like you to keep secrets from me. It's against our code," Obviously agitated.

I tactlessly chuckle, "Our code?"

"This isn't a joke! You know our code! 1. Chicks before dicks. 2. No secrets. 3. No judgment. 4. Always have each other's back. And right now you wouldn't know if I needed you or not."

"Woah! Maybe I need you right now and you're already doing what I need from you? Did you stop to consider that I need to be alone? Or maybe have something I'm dealing with? Maybe you could be my bestie that's there for me? Well? Everything isn't always about you." Fuck, I didn't mean to yell at her.

"Straight from the mouth of a spoiled trust fund baby."

I need to be straight with her, but I'm not ready. "You will always be my bestie and the ho I look up to. I will love you like my sister into eternity. I understand the code. I'm sorry I'm not there for you. I know you don't understand why I've been gone for so long. I'm dealing with something and I need to handle the situation on my own. I promise I'll tell you as soon as it's time. I need you to be patient with me," Burning tears suddenly stream down my face.

"Please tell me what's up with you."

"Soon," Mac Nut is kicking for a goal repeatedly, his response to me being upset.

"Are you in rehab? I told you not to go to the fat farm, you're not overweight. I'm going to figure this out. Wait! Are you being held against your will and watched while you are on calls, so you can't say anything because they'll kill you? That's got to be it! If I'm right, tell me how good the pineapple is there and if I'm wrong tell me the passion fruit is sour."

"You need to quit watching late night movies. I'm not being held captive."

"That's exactly what you'd say if you were being held captive."

"Are you kidding me right now?"

"Nope. I'm going to call the authorities."

"Fine. The fresh passion fruit juice is so sour that they added a sugar cane stick to it at breakfast. Is that better?"

"It'll do. Whatever's going on, please take care of yourself," followed immediately by the click of her disconnecting.

That's bad, but I'm sure she'll understand in time.

Chapter 17

Jonah

Walking up to Ashley's house I get deja-vu. I've been here so many times with differing results. The most amazing nights of my life have been spent alone with her. We've talked until the sun came up. We've spent hours naked together until we couldn't hold our eyes open any longer. She's also ignored me, told me to stay on my side of the room, and eventually given into me once I'm in her presence. This is harder. She hasn't been home in months and unless I get lucky and she answers the door, I need to find out where she is.

Lights are on and I can hear a laugh track playing on the TV. I knock hopefully and wait.

An eye investigates through the peephole, "What do you want?"

"I think it's obvious. I want Ashley."

"Sorry, she's not here."

"When will she be here?"

"I don't know."

"Where is she?"

"Not here!"

"But you do know where she is?"

"Yes."

"What's the address?"

"I'm not supposed to share that info. It's confidential."

I consider my words and go for it, "But you're going to because you don't know why she's been gone so long and somebody needs to go check on her. I promise I'll leave her alone if she asks me to when I see her in person. I'll send you a photo of her as soon as I see her."

"I can't, it's our girl code."

"I appreciate your loyalty and how you've got her back. This is different. I'm not sure what's wrong, but I think she's mistaken about me and I want to fix it. I need to fix it. I need her."

Chapter 18

Ashley

It's gotten to the point that one of the bellman helps me to the beach every day. It started out me in my big floppy hat, sunscreen, and my beach towel. That changed, one thing at a time, and now it's me in my big floppy hat, huge sunglasses that cover my whole face, sunscreen, a beach blanket, a beach towel, an umbrella, a small cooler with water, juice, and snacks (Auntie insisted), and a lounge chair. Okay, fine, I also have a direct walkie to Auntie since she found me still on the beach when she was attempting to bring me dinner and I couldn't get up off the beach. And yes, that is when the lounge chair got added to my daily excursion.

On warmer than normal days when the sun is beating down, Kala sends the bellman to bring me in from the beach during the middle of the day. She's says it's too much for me in my state and mumbles something about being sun baked. It works out fine and I end up back out on the beach to view the gorgeous sunsets.

Some days I take longer to get moving and don't make it to the sand until late afternoon. Those days may be my favorites. A different crowd on the beach that brings more activity. Local teenagers after school. Working people finishing their day and finding a spot on the sand to relax, or the perfect wave calling them to surf. The waves whip about with the wind in the late afternoon and send a visible mist to the shore. Waves over ten feet tall pound the sand at the shoreline violently, yet gracefully at the same time. The perfect symphony of strings reaching the height of their crescendo in unison. Couples wandering the sand as sunset approaches. The ocean roaring more loudly as the sun descends into the distance, changing the blue sky to warm hues of gold and orange until the horizon has devoured it completely.

As I absorb it all, a calmness comes over me and I'm ready to tell Raye about my Mac Nut. I dial her immediately, suddenly excited to share with her. She doesn't answer.

To Raye: Hey! Where are you?
Raye: Busy.
To Raye: Busy?
Raye: Yep. I've got a life, too. You don't need to know everything.

Whatever. It must not be time.

Chapter 19

Jonah

Landing in Honolulu I hope Ashley's roommate didn't give me a fake address to throw me off and get me to leave her alone. It's a chance I had to take. I need to find her. I need to be live and in person with her. I rent a car and type the address into the navigation system. I text Mighty Midge while I wait for it to load.

> To Midge: Going off the company grid.
> To Midge: Please cover me.
> Midge: How long?
> To Midge: Not sure. Let's say 24 hours.
> Midge: No problem. If possible, please check in.
> To Midge: Thank you.

The nav says she's on the North side of the island and I follow the directions, driving and taking in the tropical scenery on my way. Tropical, humid, and green everywhere. Food trucks parked along side the road with lines of people waiting. Locals with booths set up to sell their wares and fresh grown fruit.

As I get closer and the navigation says I'm only fifteen minutes away, I worry about what I'm going to find. What if she's not alone? Maybe she's with family or another man? What if she truly is done with me and I'm an idiot. None of it matters. I'm here now and I'm going to find her. I'm going to establish my presence with her and leave no questions about what I want from her. I can't believe I went off company grid when I'm so close to getting what I want.

I turn into the North Shore Shacks and wander the grounds until I find her unit. I knock on the door and nobody answers, a response I'm becoming accustomed to. I walk to the beach, taking in my surroundings. The tall palm trees swaying in the breeze. The waves calling from the ocean. This place is beauty in its natural state. The people are spread sparsely on the sand, enjoying their varied activities. I survey the beach to find a pregnant woman in a bikini lying under an umbrella, children playing in the sand at the shoreline, and college students on vacation in skimpy bikinis.

"No, no, no!" Draws my attention back to the pregnant woman. "Damn it! That 'I've fallen and I can't get up' commercial is no longer funny." She's sitting on the sand alone and unable to get up by herself. Poor lady. She shouldn't be out here as pregnant as she is, at least not by herself.

I walk towards her, and when I reach her to offer my hand—it's Ashley. I drop to my knees at her side, dumbfounded.

She stares at me shocked, "What are you doing here?"

"I'm here on a mission to find you."

"You're not supposed to find me!" Upset by my presence.

"Why did you run away?"

She glances at her belly, "Isn't it obvious?"

"You ran away because you're pregnant? Why wouldn't you stay where you'd have help?"

"For you." Tears begin to roll down her face. "I can handle this by myself and I don't want to impose on you. I don't want us to interfere with your plans. We can't be what keeps you from achieving your goals. You need to have everything you want and desire."

"You're what I've been dreaming about," I pick her up and kiss her sweetly on the lips as I carry her back to her shack.

Chapter 20

Ashley

What's happening here? He's not supposed to be here! Why am I letting him carry me? This was my world and I had it under control, well at least mostly under control. I would've figured out a way to get my ass up off the sand. I can always get Auntie Kala on the walkie if necessary.

"You can put me down now," I declare insistently.

"No."

"I can walk all by myself."

"You needed help and I'm taking advantage of the opportunity. I'm not putting you down, this way you can't run away from me. Though I doubt you can run with that huge belly anyway. Doesn't matter, I'm not taking any chances."

"Rude."

"Simply stating a fact. Are we having a boy or a girl?"

"I'm having a boy."

"You're pregnant with my child. He's my son. All I've wanted for months was you. He's an unexpected bonus."

"You don't have time for me, let alone us. Walk away and I'll never ask for anything."

He finally sets me down on the bed. He stands between me and the door, facing me while he takes a photo of me and my phone immediately rings. I ignore my phone, mostly because it's on the other side of the room and I'm having a lazy moment. I watch as he dials.

"Hey Midge."

"Checking in like I requested. Thank you."

"No. I'm quitting."

"You're the boss, but it's not the best time for that."

"Some things are more important."

"Understood. She's lucky to have you."

"She doesn't agree with you. She's a runner at this point and I'm not letting her out of my sight."

"She'll come around. You're one of the good ones. I'll follow up with you confirming your resignation."

"Thank you. Mighty to the very end Midge." I hang up.

"What did you just do?"

"I quit my job."

"You idiot."

"I'm not leaving you again. I don't want you having any confusion about how important you are to me. You're everything," He stares into my eyes unwavering. I stand to object and he grips my hips with ownership as he presses his lips to mine.

"Stop doing that!"

He kisses me again, gently and lingering. Then again with passion in his grip as he pulls me closer, stopping suddenly, and gazing down at my belly. "Tell me about our baby."

I place my hand below my bump to support it, "This is my Mac Nut. He enjoys spending time kicking my bladder. He reacts to everything I have a significant reaction to. He's strong. He relaxes when I'm resting on the beach."

"Our Mac Nut. When is he due? Does he have a name?"

"Four weeks or so, but the doctor expects him to be early. Um, Mac Nut?" Did I not make that clear?

"That's cute, like peanut or bean. Shouldn't we start calling him by his name at this point?"

I've been content, not considering the part of the process when he's actually here, "I'll think about it."

He stares at me wide-eyed, "You don't have a name chosen."

"One step at a time."

"Fair enough." His hands caress me, inspecting my shape with a different appreciation. He leans into my ear and whispers, "I've missed you. I hated not knowing where you were. I can't believe you were hiding from me." His arms wrap around me tight, "Never do it again, Ashe. Never again."

The comfort of his arms relaxes me and gives me strength I didn't know I was missing. My phone rings again and I grab it needing an escape, "Hello?"

"Why didn't you tell me you're pregnant?" Shit, Raye.

"You didn't have time for me when I called to tell you."

"Let me rephrase that. Why'd you keep it a secret for months? Did you know when you went to Hawaii?"

"Yes, I knew when I went to Hawaii. I didn't want anyone to find out. I was protecting Jonah. He can't handle the distraction of me and his job, let alone me and a baby. Best option was for him not to know. I want the best for him."

"Obviously he knows since he sent me a photo and it doesn't look like a bumpie."

"Yea, and he quit his job."

"Wow, he's slipping into the Splenda Daddy category quick."

"Anyway, he's right here listening. I'll call you when we can talk."

"Are you sure you don't have anything else you're hiding?"

"To the best of my knowledge, this makes me back in good standing with our code. Please don't share with anyone. I haven't told my mother or anybody."

"I've always got your back." She hangs up accepting me again.

I needed the break to consider my options with Jonah. He's standing there watching me as if I'm gong to make a break for it. Admittedly, he's right. I can't run. This isn't what I wanted for him. I want him to have the life he's been working for and not be tied to a family.

Chapter 21

Jonah

She's considering how she can run from me. I reach for her and pull her to me, holding her back to me with my hands on her belly. She gasps at my actions, objecting yet not pulling away. "Ashley, stop running from me and admit that you want to be with me. I want to be with you, only you." She squirms and remains quiet. "I haven't so much as offered to buy another woman a drink since I met you. You're in my head and my heart." I turn her to face me, "Nobody compares to you." I delicately trace her lips with my finger, then kiss her tenderly. I'm rewarded by her fingers in my hair and her lips asking for more. I continue to kiss her, her sweetness flooding my senses and bringing my memories of us together back to life. I slide my tongue across her lips and she opens for me, inviting me in.

Chapter 22

Ashley

What am I doing? Damn it! I've never been able to tell him no. It's his kiss. I want more. It owns me. It takes every bit of strength that I have to pull away and sit on the edge of the bed. "Are you sure you want me? This?" I ask palming my belly.

"Yes." He sits on the bed next to me and puts his arms around me. "The two most important things in the world are right here in my arms." He sits leaning his forehead to mine, "Ashe, you are everything I want." His gaze meets mine and the room gets warmer. He glides his hand up my back to my hair, wrapping my ponytail around his wrist and holding my hair taught in his hand. Controlling the angle of my neck, he devours me. His other hand explores my body from my tight round shape to my full swollen breasts. Slowly taking in each detail and change to my body. Appreciation runs through his body. His touch on my sensitive breasts, a shock to my system waking my sexual desires.

I watch as his hooded chestnut eyes get darker, "Yes, Jonah. Please."

He smiles at me and pushes his finger under the seam of my bikini bottoms, hooking them and sliding them down my legs until they fall to the floor. My sex bared to him, he caresses my thighs up to my hips and groans as he leans over me catching my scent. His hands glide up my body, palming my belly full of his baby and kissing it on his way by. He unties my bikini top and tosses it across the room leaving me naked for him. He takes time with each of my breasts, holding them with both hands, licking my areolas, kissing my nipples, and pulling my breasts into his mouth. The sensitivity is insane. Heightened in my current state, more than I could've imagined. It's hard to handle his touch, but I need him at the same time—I need more. He makes a line of kisses from my breasts to my wet heat, and stops to worship. His tongue laps at my clit slowly over and over. This is how he started every time we were together, always my pleasure first. There's something different this time. Maybe it's simply me and my hormones. The way his hands hold my body as if he's taking care of me. The depth of his eyes as he dives into mine like he's searching my heart and soul, or finding the path to our future. His luxurious tongue taking his time like I'm a luscious dessert that he wants to last. Is this truly more? Maybe he loves me the way I love him. I shake as he caresses and kisses me, from his contact alone. It's been so long since I've been touched like this, but again this is different, this is more, is this what I've been waiting for? His hands hold my hips while he continues to lick me, he drags his tongue down my seam and back up to my clit. He starts down my seam again and I grab onto his head, holding him in place to suck and nibble at my clit. He groans at my actions, digging his fingers into my hips, and holding me down while he makes me come repeatedly. Bucking at his mouth uncontrollably and crying out his name while I squeeze his head with my thighs. He continues on and on with his magic tongue until I'm sated.

His hands explore my body, I hear his shorts hit the ground and his cock is hard against my leg. "Ashe, is this okay?"

"Yes."

He starts to push into me and changes his mind. He rolls me onto my side and slides a pillow underneath my belly for support. He spoons me from behind, holding me with his arms around me and pushes into me. "Oh, Jonah. I need you." He pushes and pulls slowly, over and over. I moan in pleasure.

"I need you, too. It's been torture without you. Promise you'll never run from me again. Tell me you're mine. Ashe, are you mine?" He speaks sweetly into my ear, kissing my neck.

"I ran to protect you because I love you, so yes I'm yours." He squeezes me tighter and continues to stroke in and out of my wet heat.

He pulls out and moves to lie in front of me. Facing me on his side, he places his hand on my cheek and gazes into my eyes, "Nothing will ever be as important as you. I love you, Ashley."

I fall asleep in his arms and wake to his phone ringing early in the morning. Well, early in the morning Hawaiian time. He grabs it groggily, "Hello?"

Chapter 23

Jonah

"Good morning, boss."

"I quit yesterday, Midge."

"About that, when I turned in your resignation they made a counter-offer."

"What are you talking about? I quit."

"Apparently they were waiting for you to be human and not work like a machine."

"Midge, it's very early here. What are you telling me?"

"They are offering you the CEO position."

"Not interested."

"Jonah, this is what you've been working for."

"It's not important anymore. I'm not going to be gone for work. I want to be home. I'm going to spend the next month with my pregnant woman and then I'm going to spend the next three months with her and my baby boy. If they want me after that, I'll consider traveling if I can take them with me."

"I already negotiated the next six months off for you with no more than thirty minutes of meetings per day via Skype, and a signing bonus. Oh, and you get to keep me and give me a raise."

"How is this possible?"

"HR said you are perfect for the CEO position, but the company overall has been lacking a human element that you now bring to the table."

"It sounds unbelievable, I'll need to talk to Ashley. It's up to her. I'll get back to you next week."

"They're giving you two weeks to respond. Take the whole time. I'll hold down the fort."

"Thank you, Mighty Midge."

"That's what I'm here for. Congrats, Jonah."

"I didn't take the job yet."

"You already took a much more important position, dad." She hangs up.

I turn to Ashley, "Did you catch all that?"

"It sounds like you get everything you want."

"It's up to you. I'm not traveling without you and Mac. I'm not accepting the position without your approval. I meant it when I said you are the most important. I'm not losing you. I'll do anything for you, my everything." I kiss her, claiming her completely as I fall back into bed with the woman of my dreams.

Read Raye's story... The Panty Thief

From USA Today Bestselling Author Naomi Springthorp comes a romantic comedy with heat, a cat, and a hottie named Truck.

I've always had my best friend. She's the sister I chose and with me for life. She's also the only roommate I've ever had. Everything was perfect—until she popped out a baby.

I have to move out. I can't sleep in my own bed and I'm waking up everyone in the house when I get home from the club. Nobody wants to hear a crying baby at 3am. Especially when I just left my conquest for the night begging for more.

Crashing at my ex's while I apartment hunt is only a temporary solution.

Now, my bestie is forcing me to have a house warming party—and if I know her at all, she has an ulterior motive.

There's a new hot chick in my building.
She's put together and her attitude is off the charts.

I didn't expect her to be a cat lady.

I'm not into her. Women are trouble.

Her scent lingers in the hallway and drives me nuts.

Hitting it in my own building? Not going to happen. It's hard enough to hide being the owner from the tenants. That's extra drama I don't want or need.

The warm sunbeam every afternoon. My favorite treats. They fed me well at the rescue house and the other cats learned I was in charge early on.

Naomi Springthorp

The woman with the screaming infant who picked me up was not ideal. However, my new maid and I will get along just fine. She just doesn't know it yet.

An excerpt from The Panty Thief

Truck

...It's a warm day, so I pull my t-shirt off and hang it out the back of my surf trunks before I get to work. I love the warmth of the sun beating on my bare skin, it's one of the reasons I settled in OC. Nothing like the Southern California sun and sand. I could've chosen anywhere, but this place has always called to me.

I dig the hole and get the sign planted. It really is an eyesore, but I chose it on purpose. I want it to be seen. I need to keep the building rented out at 100%, so I can work on purchasing another building.

"Nice tan baby. Turn around and show us those abs," a convertible full of women yell at me as they drive by. Which reminds me of the other lesson I learned at the first building: Don't hit it in the building. In fact, don't flirt with it, don't buy it coffee, don't even gaze at it out of the corner of my eye. Keep women I'm interested in off the property completely. No exceptions, not even for one-night stands. Shit, especially not one-night stands. No crazy hos in the building, not as tenants or visitors or hook-ups of any kind.

I stop in Vin's office on my way to my apartment after getting the sign in place, "Sign has been installed."

"I assumed so. I've had three calls already and have the first applicant scheduled for her interview," he checks me from head to foot. "Is that how you presented yourself to the world as this building's maintenance man?"

"Is there a problem?" I glare at him wondering if he has forgotten who signs his paycheck and provides him with his apartment.

"No Sir. Not a single one. MMM, mmm, mmm!" Vin grins deviously.

"I'm sorry?" I side-eye him.

"The women who are applying have obviously seen you shirtless out there showing the world your gorgeous self," Vin says with attitude.

"Is that a problem?" I ask.

"Nope. I'm raising the rent," he giggles.

"I don't dislike the idea of more money, but what's your motivation?"

"Well, everyone knows you pay extra for a view," he states as a clear-cut fact.

"But..."

"I'm going to have to come up with more jobs for you to do shirtless," he grins.

"I'm not the attraction here. Rent the apartments. Stop trying to hook me up." I hope he's listening to me.

An excerpt from The Panty Thief

"Maybe take some photos for future reference to use for marketing," he continues with his smart-ass ideas.

I turn and leave his office before he comes up with something else for me to do.

Read The Panty Thief at:
https://books2read.com/pantythief

About the Author

USA Today Bestselling Author Naomi Springthorp is a born and raised Southern California girl who believes that life has a soundtrack and half of each year should be spent cheering for her favorite baseball team. She loves music and spending time with her feline fur babies.

Naomi writes Baseball Romance, Romantic Comedies, Contemporary Romance, and 90s Throwbacks—all with heat and sometimes a little sweet.

Sign-up for Naomi's newsletter at
www.naomispringthorp.com/sign-up
to get updates on everything she has going on.

Join Naomi's reader group at https://www.facebook.com/groups/naomisreaders for fun, baseball, and hotties.

facebook.com/naomithewriter

instagram.com/naomispringthorp

amazon.com/author/naomispringthorp

bookbub.com/authors/naomi-springthorp

goodreads.com/naomithewriter

twitter.com/naomithewriter

pinterest.com/naomispringthorp

tiktok.com/@naomispringthorp

Also by Naomi Springthorp

An All About the Diamond Romance

The Sweet Spot

King of Diamonds

Diamonds in Paradise (a novella)

Star-Crossed in the Outfield

The Closer (a novella)

Falling For Prince (A Short Stop)

Up to Bat

Betting on Love

Just a California Girl

Jacks

Novellas and standalone novels

Muffin Man (a novella)

Finally in Focus (a novella)

Confessions of an Online Junkie

Anthologies & Box Sets

Sacrifice for Love

Storybook Pub

Storybook Pub Christmas Wishes

Storybook Pub 2

Young Crush

Hate to Want You

Tricks, Treats, & Teasers

Caught Under the Mistletoe

Game On

Imperfect Date

Hopelessly Devoted

Made in the USA
Middletown, DE
29 June 2024

56509616R00047